World of Rea

A 3-in-1 Listen-Along Reader

DISNEY · PIXAR

Three Tales of Speed

DISNEP PRESS

Los Angeles • New York

First Paperback Edition, May 2017
1 3 5 7 9 10 8 6 4 2

ISBN 978-1-4847-9951-2
FAC-029261-17076
Library of Congress Control Number: 2016938192

Printed in the United States of America

For more Disney Press fun, visit www.disneybooks.com

SUSTAINABLE
FORESTRY
INITIATIVE
Certified Sourcing
www.sfiprogram.org
SFI-01415

Written by

Brooke Dworkin

Illustrated by the

Disney Storybook Art Team

Lightning McQueen is in a race.
Chick Hicks and The King
are racing, too.
The three cars tie.

There will be a
tiebreaker race.
It will be in California
in one week.

On the way to California,
Lightning gets lost.
He is scared.
He drives too fast.

Lightning's fast driving
destroys the road.
He gets tangled
in some wires.

Lightning ends up in
Radiator Springs.
He cannot leave until
he fixes the road.

Lightning fixes the road.
He does a bad job.
The judge tells him to
do it again.

Lightning does not want to
fix the road.
He wants to race.
He makes a deal with the judge.

The judge is named Doc.
He and Lightning race.
Lightning loses.
Doc makes him fix the road.

The next day, Doc finds Lightning
working on his turns.
He is having trouble
driving on dirt.

Doc helps Lightning.
He tells him to turn left
if he wants
to go right.

Lightning goes back to
fixing the road.
He is starting to like the town.

Lightning has fun with
Mater the tow truck.
He goes for a drive with Sally.

Lightning goes to see Doc.
He sees a Piston Cup
in Doc's garage.
Doc was a race car!

Doc tells Lightning that
he had an accident.
By the time he could race again,
he had been replaced.

The road is done.
It is time for Lightning
to go to California.

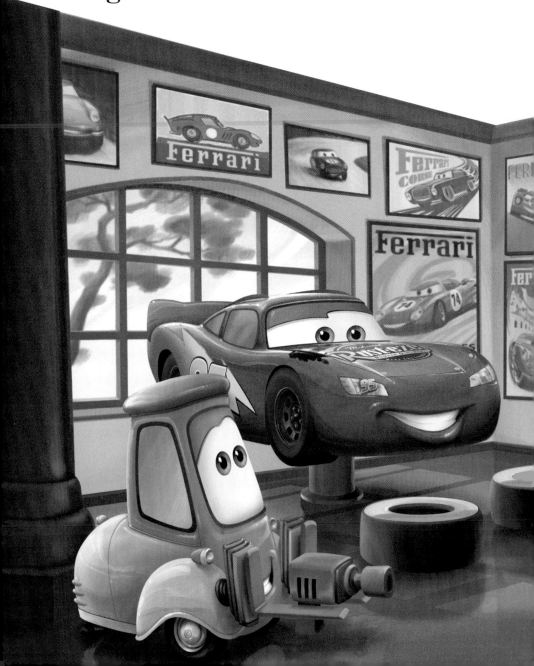

First he goes to
all the shops
in town.

Lightning goes for a
nighttime drive.
He will miss all of
his new friends.

It is time for
the big race.
Lightning cannot focus.
He misses his friends.

Lightning hears a voice.
It is Doc!

His friends came to
cheer him on.

Lightning gets back
in the race.
He uses the moves
his friends taught him.

He drives backward.
He turns left
to go right.
Soon he is winning.

Chick Hicks does not
want to lose.
He crashes into The King.

The King flips over.
He cannot
finish the race.

Lightning helps The King.
He pushes him
over the finish line.

Chick Hicks wins the race.
The crowd cheers for Lightning.
He is a hero!

Lightning goes back to
Radiator Springs.
He has found a place
to call home.

Racing Days

Written by
Brooke Dworkin

Illustrated by the
Disney Storybook Art Team

Lightning McQueen is
a race car.
His friend Doc
used to race, too.

Doc has a racing school.
He teaches his students
how to climb out of holes.

He teaches them
how to drive
in the dirt.

Chick Hicks has a racing school, too. He teaches his students how to cheat.

Chick and Doc decide to
race against each other.
They will have three races
to see which school is best.

The first race starts.
Lightning is racing with
his friend Mater.
Chick's partner is named Switcher.

Lightning takes the lead.
Chick is close behind.

Chick tells Switcher to take care of Lightning.

Switcher uses his turbo boost.
He pulls ahead of Lightning.
He spills oil on the road.
Lightning slips!

Switcher takes the lead.
That makes Chick angry.
He wants to win.
He knocks Switcher into the dirt.

Lightning and Mater work
as a team.
Mater weaves in front of Chick.
Lightning crosses the finish line.

The next race is
in the desert.
Lightning and Sarge race
as a team.

The flag drops.
Chick and Sarge take off.

Chick drops bolts
on the ground.
He wants Sarge to crash.

Chick watches Sarge.
He does not see a cactus.
Chick is the one to crash.

Chick cheats again.
He moves the sign
showing which way to drive.

Chick's partner drives
the wrong way.
Lightning wins the race!

The next race is
by the sea.
Lightning is racing against
a pink car named Candice.

Candice likes being famous.
She likes having
her picture taken.

Lightning trains with Sally.
He turns in the dirt.

He gets used to
the bright sun.

The race starts.
Candice uses her mirror
to blind Lightning.
He cannot see.

Lightning catches up
to Candice.
She sprays him
with sand.

Lightning drives
off the road.
He is losing
the race.

Candice nears the
finish line.
Her fans take
pictures of her.

The lights blind Candice.
She cannot see.
Lightning passes her.
He wins the race.

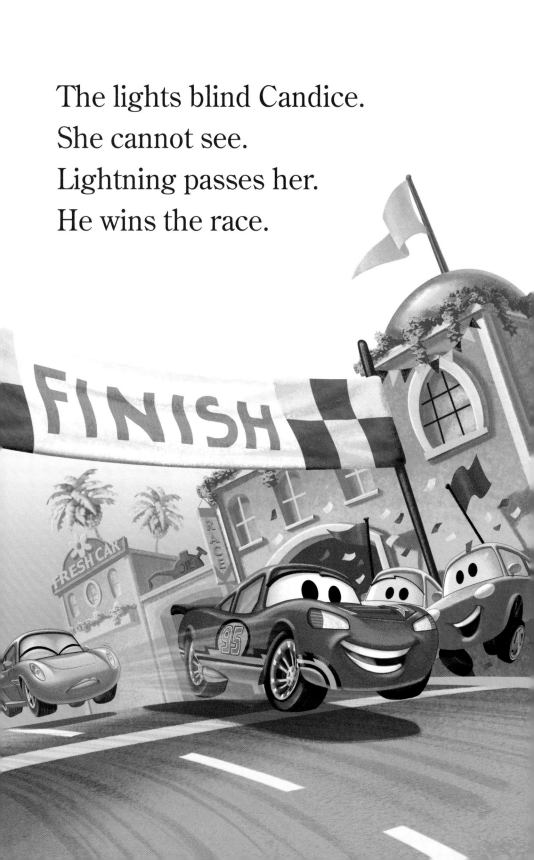

Lightning won all three races.
Doc's school is
the best school!

Rally to the Finish

Written by
Brooke Dworkin

Illustrated by the
Disney Storybook Art Team

Lightning McQueen is
a race car.
His best friend is
Mater the tow truck.

Lightning and his friends are
going to a race.
It is in
the Black Forest.

Lightning's friend Max greets them
at the airport.
He is glad they came.

Lightning talks to
the other racers.
Raoul thinks he
will win the race.

Mater does not agree.
He tells the other cars that
Lightning will win.

Lightning tells Mater that he
wants to practice in the forest.
An old car hears him.

The car tells Mater
there is a monster
in the forest.

Lightning is not scared.
He does not think
there is a monster.

Lightning goes into the forest.
Mater goes with him.
Mater is still scared.

Lightning and Mater
race each other.

They go over
an old bridge.

They go through
a small stream.

Mater is having fun.
Lightning is, too.

Lightning goes left.
He thinks Mater
is behind him.

Mater goes right.
He thinks Lightning
is behind him.

Mater sees a scary tree.
He thinks it
is the monster!

Lightning hears Mater scream.
He rushes to
save his friend.

Lightning finds Mater.
The friends find the road.
They follow the road
back to town.

Lightning still does not think
there is a monster.
Mater does not agree.
He is sure there is a monster.

Soon it is time
for the race.
Mater asks Lightning
not to race.

He is scared
of the monster.
The other racers hear Mater.
Now they are scared, too.

The flag drops.
The cars take off.
Lightning is in the lead.

The racers hear
a strange sound.
They think it
is the monster!

The racers speed
down the road.

They are scared
of the shadows.

The racers go
over the bridge.
They go through the stream.

They drive fast.
They want to get
out of the woods!

The racers cross
the finish line
at the same time.
It is a four-way tie!

The racers thank Mater.
They were so scared
they drove faster than ever!